The Muddle-headed
WOMBAT
and the Invention

RUTH PARK

Illustrated by NOELA YOUNG

ANGUS
& ROBERTSON

A division of HarperCollins *Publishers*

What a very hot summer it was! The sun burned like a bushfire, and all the world became brown and papery. The Big Bush creek sank lower and lower. Soon it would be only a necklace of muddy pools. Animals that ate grass looked thin. Animals that ate tender leaves and shoots had to travel for miles before they found enough to eat.

The Muddle-headed Wombat and his best friend Mouse saved bread crusts, carrot tops and fruit skins for the hungry bandicoots. But they still ate the sleeves of Wombat's cardigan when he left it outside one night. Wombat was annoyed.

"Those bandicoots are terribubble, Mouse, treely ruly they are," he complained. "I'll never get another cardigan with so many useful holes."

"Cheer up, Wombat," said Mouse. "Because the postman has just left a letter from Tabby Cat!"

Now, Tabby Cat, who was their second-best friend, was having a holiday in the city with his sporty Uncle Bobtail. Mouse and Wombat tried to be glad for Tabby's sake, but they missed him. Besides, it was hard not to be envious of a cat who, while they were roasting and toasting in Big Bush, was having such an exciting time.

"Oooh, that Tabby!" said Mouse. "Just listen to this, Wombat. Dear Mouse and Wombat—"

"That's me!" chuckled Wombat. "Read that bit again, Mouse, it's so loverly."

"Dear Mouse and Wombat," began Mouse.

"Of course, the dear Mouse bit isn't me," explained Wombat. But after he had been bitten on the toe, he was fairly quiet.

"Now then," glared Mouse. And it read: "Dear Mouse and Wombat, what do you think, your brilliant pussy has learnt to drive a car! I drove all the way up a hill, and then I drove backwards down the hill because I had forgotten to put the brakes on. Oh, Mouse, your little eyes would beam if you could see me in my gorgeous new clothes, the very latest, *latest* gear, Mouse! And I have had my tail done!"

"Whatever does 'tail done' mean, Mouse, eh, what?" asked Wombat.

"Curled, chopped off, or dyed green, I don't know and I don't care!" snapped Mouse, who loved pretty clothes and wished it had a few for itself. And it read on crossly: "But the best thing is that Uncle Bobtail took me for a ride in a plane—isn't that thrilling, Wombat? Don't you wish you were handsome and clever and lucky like me?"

"I do, too," said Wombat sadly. "Why don't we have loverly holidays like Tabby, Mouse, eh, why?"

"Because we have the wrong kind of uncles," said Mouse.

Wombat thought. "I don't think I have any kind of uncles. How horri-bubble! Unless the Clever Old Man who lives in the lily lagoons is my uncle. Is he, Mouse?"

"Of course he isn't," said Mouse snappily. "He isn't a wombat, is he? He's a magician. He's an old, old human. Ohhh!" said Mouse suddenly:

"I'm so hot and cross and jealous of poor Tabby! What will make me feel better? I know, I'll have a shower."

Mouse's shower was a dripping garden tap. Very soon, there it was in its tiny blue bathing-suit, with a drop standing on top of its head like a big round diamond. Then the drop rolled down and hung on the end of Mouse's long pink nose, and then it splashed in a tiny pool on Mouse's toes. Oh, it was beautiful!

"I wish I had a shower too," said Wombat. "Why am I such a big animal?
Oh, I'm so hot, I'm boiling, treely ruly I am, Mouse." Then he had an idea.
"I know what I'll do. I'll take off my skin and play in my bones."

And he tried to get his short, stout paws up around the back of his neck.

"What *are* you doing, Wombat?" asked Mouse, coming out of its shower
and wringing out its whiskers.

"I'm looking for my zipper," he explained.

"Silly," said Mouse. "Your skin doesn't have a zipper!"

Wombat looked clever. "Then how did I get into it in the first place, eh?"

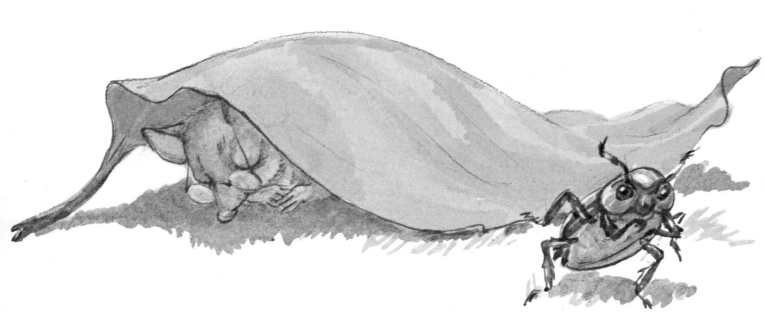

"Oh, do stop bothering, Wombat," wailed Mouse. "I'm going to have a little sleep," and it crept into the green cave under a big fallen leaf. But other people had had the same idea. Mouse exchanged a few slaps with a praying mantis, fiercely rolled a little beetle out into the sun, and then dragged away a small snail. It flopped down and tried to sleep. But cicadas were shrilling, and bushflies were humming, and Wombat kept jabbering to himself.

"I know!" he said. "Maybe I have a button. On top of my head!"

Under its leaf, Mouse sighed.

Wombat felt around carefully. There were quite a few lumps on top of his head, mostly where things had fallen on him. But there was no button. He was dismayed.

"Just suppose I needed my fur drycleaned, or mended. I could never get it off. How terribubble!"

Mouse crept out once more, patted his paw and squeaked soothingly: "Don't worry, poor old Wombat. I'm here to look after things like that. Now, what can you do that will keep you quiet until lunchtime? I know. Why don't you work on your cubby?"

Wombat had been building a cubby house for ages. He was always pulling it to pieces and changing it and kicking it when it fell down. Now he gave a great hoot of joy that almost made Mouse jump out of its toenails.

"I've had a horribubbly good idea, Mouse!" he shouted. "You know how Tabby had a ride in a plane? I'm going to do something betterer! I'm going to turn my cubby into a plane, a real one!"

"Oh, what fun," said Mouse drowsily.

"And then I can take you and the koalas and the wallabies and even those mean horribubble bandicoots to the lily lagoons for a swim! Aren't I a kind wombat!"

"Oh, you *are*!" said Mouse, and it fell down under the cool green leaf once more and went to sleep.

All the hot morning Wombat hammered and sawed and pushed and pulled things about. He hung his cardigan over a bush and the bandicoots ate the whole back out of it, and he didn't notice. He was so excited and pleased about his flying cubby that he chattered about it all through lunch. And at last little Mouse understood that Wombat thought his flying cubby would really fly. Mouse was sad for its friend.

"Oh, my! But a mouse must tell the truth. Your plane won't really fly, Wombat dear."

Wombat stuck his lip out. " 'Course it will! It's a terribubbly good plane."

"I know, but it's only pretend, and it hasn't any engine, you see," explained Mouse. "Here you are, have a snail sandwich!"

"Don't want a snail sandwich! My plane will so fly! You'll be sorry when you see me flying over Big Bush, mean old Mouse."

And he jammed his hat over his eyes, gave Mouse a fierce glare, and trundled out. He scrambled into his flying cubby, and tugged a piece of string that was meant to start the propeller. He pushed a bit of wood that was supposed to make the plane begin to roll across the lawn. But nothing happened.

"Oh, don't be disappointed, poor Wombat!" cried kind Mouse.

"Go on, hurry up and start, you silly old plane!" roared Wombat. "Do you want a horribubble kick?"

Bang! Clang! Crash! Still the plane wouldn't move. Wombat gave it one last great kick, and a wheel fell off. Then he thumped the propeller, and it flew up and bounced away down the garden path. Wombat threw himself down and kicked his stout legs and made such a brokenhearted noise that Mouse climbed up on his head and sat there, stroking his ears and not saying "I told you so."

"I knew all the time it wouldn't go, Mouse," choked Wombat. "Because you said it wouldn't, and you're always right, and I'm just a muddle-headed wombat. But I *wanted* my plane to fly so that I could take you and all the poor hot bush animals for a swim! I treely ruly did, Mouse."

Just at this moment, who should be coming up the bush track but Tabby Cat? He was very hot and tired, but excited because of the wonderful surprise he was going to give his dear friends Mouse and Wombat. Of course, he wanted the surprise to be as wonderful as possible, so before he got to the gate, he put down his suitcase, took out his pocket mirror and had a peep to see if his new green velvet cap was looking just as fashionable as it had in the city.

"And it looks gorgeous, and so do I!" said Tabby. "Oh, what a vision of a cat! That vest with the long fringe! Those jeans with the fish-shaped patches! My chain and pendant! And, best of all, my marvellous, marvellous tail!"

He could hardly wait for his friends to see and admire him, so he bounded onwards, and arrived on the lawn just in time to see Mouse comforting poor Wombat, His friends could not believe their eyes.

"That can't be you, Tabby," said Mouse.

"Because you're having a loverly holiday in town with Uncle Bobtail," said Wombat.

"No, you lucky animals," said Tabby. "It's really wonderful me. I came home early because I missed my little Mouse. I even missed that person there, the one with red eyes and his mouth open."

Wombat said in a loud whisper: "Mouse, there's something sticking on Tabby's poor old head."

"That's my new cap, the very latest style!" squalled Tabby.

"And he must be very poor, because his coat is all raggy, and just look at his jeans, patched all over!" said Mouse, quite shocked.

"And just look, Mouse, how awfullous!" cried Wombat. "Something terribubble has happened to his tail, it's all kinks!"

"It's been permed, you muddle-head!" screeched Tabby. "And everyone in the city thought it looked super. And it does, it does, it does!"

"H'm," said Mouse thoughtfully. "But just a bit possumy, perhaps, Tabby dear."

"If he left it all night in a bucket of boiling water it might get better," said helpful Wombat.

It took hours and hours for Mouse to apologise to Tabby, and make him glad that he'd come home early after all. But when he'd cheered up and forgiven them, he unpacked his luggage and gave them the presents he had kindly brought. Mouse's was a silver chain with a locket that contained a photograph of Tabby. The locket bent Mouse right to the ground, but as Mouse pointed out, though the present was perhaps a little heavy for so small an animal, it would look splendid as a picture on the bedroom wall.

Wombat's present was a book called *101 Things a Young Wombat Can Make*. Wombat was so excited about it that, long after Tabby had gone to bed, poor Mouse was still reading bits of the book out to its friend.

"Here, wake up, Mouse! What's this thing, Mouse? Open your eyes, Mouse! This thing with a kind of loverly cruncher, what's that, eh?"

"That's for squashing vegetables," yawned Mouse. "Would you like to make that tomorrow, Wombat?"

"No, won't make that. I've got plenty of things for squashing up vegetabubbles already. They're called teeth. And I don't want to make that, and I don't like *that*, and *that*'s a terribubbly silly kind of thing. But I like *that*! Wake up, Mouse. Mouse, see that thing? First of all in the morning I'll have my breakwuss, and then I'll make that and it will be my Invention!"

Mouse was very thankful to be allowed to go to bed at last. Next morning at eight o'clock, it was still in its matchbox bed, and Tabby was still fast asleep. He was tired after his long trip from the city. When they awoke, the sun was burning yellow, the leaves hung still, thirsty birds were quarrelling around Mouse's shower, and the ratty faces of bandicoots and anteaters were peering hopefully in at the kitchen door.

Sounds of hammering came from the garden, where Wombat was finishing off his Invention.

Tabby scornfully walked around it. "Whatever is it?"

"Don't know," said Wombat cheerfully. "It might squash vegetabubbles, and it might be a useful something that takes people for rides."

And he fixed on another wheel.

"You wouldn't catch a cat making an invention like *that*," said Tabby haughtily.

"I don't care what it is," said Mouse admiringly. "I think it's beautiful. And Wombat is the smartest wombat in the whole of Big Bush for making it."

Wombat fixed on the fourth wheel, and looked at his Invention with pride. "One of these days we'll find out what it treely ruly is, Mouse. But this morning I think it's a sort of a kind of a billycart."

Mouse clasped its paws in excitement. "Oh, if only someone knew how to drive it, we could pack a picnic lunch and go to the lily lagoons for an outing after all! Oh, what fun it would be!"

Tabby preened his whiskers. "You forget, little Mouse, that while your brilliant pussy was in the city he learned how to drive. And if I can drive a car, I can drive an Invention."

He took charge at once. Mouse was sent flying to fix the lunch, Wombat to carry it. Tabby himself put on his finest city clothes, to give the bush animals a treat.

"They're bound to come out and stare. Cheer their little heads off, I expect," he said. "Do hurry up, Wombat. Don't keep my admirers waiting!"

It was true that Tabby drove the Invention very well. However, he went faster and faster, and Mouse felt a little nervous.

"Hello, hello!" shouted Tabby to a crowd of bandicoots and wallabies huddled goggle-eyed beside the track. "Aren't I a fantastic driver?"

"Stop!" roared Wombat. "I want to give them some of my sandwiches!"

But Tabby couldn't stop—because Wombat had forgotten to give his Invention any brakes.

It flashed down the track. It whizzed around corners. The scrub flickered past. The tall trees looked like a fence!

"My!" gasped Mouse, holding on to its sun-hat with one paw and Wombat's whiskers with the other. Wombat cheered Tabby onwards, enjoying every moment. And Tabby was wonderful. He held tight to the steering wheel, dodged a tree, ran down a slope so fast that everything was blurred and splashed safely into a little creek that lived in a gully so dark and deep that it still had running water.

"Wheee!" shouted Mouse. It hopped up and down excitedly as the Invention bumped down the creek, shot over a little waterfall and came gently to a stop at last in the tall, coarse water-grass that fringed the lily lagoons.

"We're safe," said Tabby in wonder. "We're floating."

"Now we know what the Invention is," beamed Mouse.

"It's a billyboat," said Wombat. "I always knew it would be something terribubbly useful."

"It's all too much for a delicate pussy," said Tabby. "I'm going to faint."

"If you do," said Mouse sternly, "Wombat will put a cold frog on your forehead."

And indeed it was no time for fainting. The billyboat did not leak a drop, for Wombat had built it very well. Mouse's nose was pale with excitement.

"If you got a long stick, Wombat, and pushed us along," it said, "we could explore the lily lagoons. We could have an adventure, Tabby. Just think."

"Adventures are all right for strong fearless mice," said Tabby. "But I'm a delicate little cat. Just look, all the waves in my tail have gone straight with fright. I shall just sit on the shore with the lunch and wait till you and Wombat get back."

But it was too late.

Wombat had seized a floating stick and given a push, and the billyboat slid out over the deeper water. The dry weather had steamed away some of the shallow lagoons. Here and there the thick stems of waterlilies lay withered and limp on the hot mud. Reeds had died. Frogs gasped in the cooler water under the mangrove roots. But where the little creek plunged into the lagoon there was a deeper, winding channel.

"I've a wonderful idea," squeaked Mouse. "Now that we're in the lily lagoons in this useful billyboat, let's go and find the Clever Old Man and ask him to say a rain spell and end the drought!"

"The magician!" said Wombat. "The one who isn't my uncle!"

"No, thank you very much," said Tabby. "Goodbye, all."

As he said this he tried to jump from the billyboat, but as quick as a wink Wombat grabbed him and stuffed him into the picnic basket.

They could hear him in there, complaining away into the sandwiches. Mouse, all afire with its great idea, sprang to the edge of the billyboat and looked eagerly about for the Clever Old Man's house.

But where was it? Mouse knew that it was built on a floating island of reeds and fallen branches that had knitted themselves into a kind of leafy raft. The wind blew it here and there—sometimes into deep water amongst the mudbanks, sometimes up on to the swampy shore. It was such a bush-coloured little house that it seemed part of the lagoons itself.

Tabby cheered up.

"Of course Mouse won't find the Clever Old Man," he said to himself, and he popped out of the picnic basket, brushed bits of snail sandwich and beetle biscuit off his jeans, arranged his fringe and his velvet cap, and looked cockily around.

"Silly old Wombat, you believed I really was afraid, didn't you! What a muddle-head you are!"

"There it is, there's the little house!" said Wombat, and Tabby shot back into the picnic basket in a flash.

"That cat!" said Mouse.

They slid up to the Clever Old Man's house. It looked just like a huge bird's nest. The door was open and there he was, asleep on a mat of reeds. Wombat gave him a poke with the stick, and he sat up angrily and sent a blue streak of lightning whizzing through the roof. Mouse jumped. It longed to get inside Wombat's hat before it was turned into a tadpole. But it made itself be brave.

"Please, Clever Old Man," it squeaked in a trembling voice, "we're sorry to wake you up but . . ."

The Clever Old Man rattled his broken cup necklace angrily.

"Go away!" he croaked. "I hate rats."

Mouse's nose turned hot and pink. "I am *not* a rat," it said. "I'm a mouse. And I came here with Wombat and Tabby because the drought has gone on for ages, and all the bush birds and animals are in *great* trouble."

"Because there's nothing left to eat, you silly old Clever Old Man!" roared Wombat, losing his temper and pounding on the picnic basket so that the lid nearly jammed Tabby's tail.

"Oh my, he'll turn us all into frogs or something," thought Mouse in terror, but it squeaked up bravely: "So we've come to ask you to say a rainmaking spell and end the drought."

But the Clever Old Man just jangled his necklace—though that was better than the blue lightning, Mouse thought.

"No, I won't say a rain spell," said the Clever Old Man crossly. "I like the hot weather because it's good for my rheumatism. Now, go away."

Meanwhile Tabby Cat had been peeping at the Clever Old Man through the chinks in the picnic basket. He saw that the magician wasn't at all well-dressed.

"That draggy old skirt or whatever it is," thought Tabby scornfully. "Not a bit smart! And that necklace—oh, miaow! And those mangy feathers in his hair—a trendy puss like me wouldn't be seen dead in them."

Suddenly the lid whipped open, and Wombat fished Tabby out by the tail.

" 'Scuse me, Tab. Mouse thinks the Clever Old Man might like the lunch for a present. Stop clawing, Tab, it's terribubble manners. Now then, Clever Old Man, see what we have here, loverly sandwiches, and carrots, and mosquito biscuits for Mouse, and some rock cakes, though they aren't made with real rocks, I don't know why. So if we give you that for a terribubbly nice present will you make a spell?"

"Please, please, Clever Old Man!" pleaded Mouse.

The Clever Old Man stretched out a skinny arm. "I'll have that."

"You don't mean our Tabby Cat?" trembled Mouse.

"You can't have wonderful me!" squalled Tabby.

"No, because he's our friend!" said Wombat, clutching Tabby chokingly to his chest. "He's not much, but he's all we have!"

The Clever Old Man sent a short sizzle of lightning darting across the lagoon. "I don't want him," he croaked, "I want his clothes."

"Naow!" yelled Tabby. He tried to climb back into the basket, he tried to jump up into a tree. He fell down on the deck of the billyboat and drummed his paws.

"Oh, be quiet, Tabby!" scolded Mouse. "What manners! Now then, Clever Old Man, do you promise faithfully to make a rain spell? Enough rain to make things grow again, mind you."

"I promise," said the Clever Old Man, his eyes glistening with joy as he looked at Tabby's beautiful town outfit.

And in no time at all Wombat was poling away from the Clever Old Man's floating house, and Tabby Cat, clad in a draggy old skirt, a broken cup necklace and a few mangy feathers, was sulking dreadfully.

"I'll never forgive you, Mouse," he said. "Never. And as for that dreadful Wombat!"

"But Tabby," coaxed Mouse, "when the rain comes you'll be the hero of Big Bush!"

Tabby sneered. "Foolish Mouse!" he said. "He won't make a spell. He was just pretending . . ."

There was a great crack of thunder.

". . . but on the other paw," added Tabby hastily "a cat always likes to help his friends, of course."

A raindrop splashed on Wombat's hat.

"My!" said Mouse. "I didn't think he'd say the spell right away."

Wombat and his friends stared at the sky. One moment it was blue. The next it was dark. Clouds marched across the sky, grey as smoke. Lightning twinkled amongst them.

"Quick, get into my hat, Mouse, you'll get horribubbly wet!" said Wombat.

"Why aren't *I* invited into your hat?" complained Tabby. "Why are people so mean to cats?"

Wombat hurried the billyboat along as fast as he could. The rain poured down until the level of the lagoons began to rise, gurgling and brown. The mudflats were soon awash, and then the water covered them completely. The dead dry grass clumps swam in the water like mops. Even inside Wombat's hat Mouse got wet, for his was a leaky hat. Tabby was furious.

"It's all your fault, you Mouse!" he caterwauled. "What a cruel thought-less Mouse to ask for rain so that its own dear cat gets soaking wet! I'm wet right through my fur. I'm wet through to *me*!"

By this time Wombat had climbed out of the billyboat and was trudging along pushing it. He *was* glad when at last the billyboat slid up on land and skidded along on its wheels.

"But I'm lost," he said. "And I'm tired and I'm wet and I'm terribubbly hungry!"

So then Tabby felt ashamed, and he helped Wombat turn the billyboat upside down. It made a fine cubby. And there they stayed, dry and comfort-able, and ate their lunch while the rain poured down, soaking Big Bush as it hadn't been soaked in months.

Tabby told them all about his holiday, and Mouse and Wombat enjoyed the hearing as much as Tabby had enjoyed the doing.

All the time the creeks were gurgling; the half-dead leaves were uncurling and turning green; the grass was growing!

The drought was over. Tabby Cat became the hero of the bush. Not being a shy cat, he told everyone how he had bravely given up all his new clothes to the Clever Old Man so that he would say a rain spell. He became famous!

"I expect I shall get a medal," he said. "I shall have my picture in the newspapers! Anything might happen to a marvellous cat like me!"

Mouse saw the way Wombat was looking. What might happen to marvellous Tabby, it feared, was that his friend Wombat might sit on him and squash him flatter than a postcard.

And it *did* happen.